and the
Rugby Match

To Dad and John who taught me that life is
too short to be anything but happy.

'Children are made readers on the laps
of their parents.'

Emilie Buchwald

If you would like to find out more about Tanya James
and Petra Brown, take a look online:
www.gomer.co.uk/authors/tanyajames.html
www.petrab.co.uk

Sid
and the
Rugby Match

Tanya L. James

Illustrated by
Petra Brown

Pont

First published in 2015 by Pont Books, an imprint of
Gomer Press, Llandysul, Ceredigion, SA44 4JL
www.gomer.co.uk

ISBN 978 1 84851 978 7

A CIP record for this title is available from the British Library.

This book is published with the financial support of the Welsh Books Council.

Printed and bound in Wales at Gomer Press, Llandysul, Ceredigion

Chapter One

It was a windy autumn day in the village of Cwmhendy.

Sid sat and watched as Dad gathered the hundreds of fallen leaves in the garden. Dad used a long rake to drag them into a huge golden-brown pile. Sid wondered to himself why that big mound of leaves had to be right on top of where he'd left his best red ball. What a nuisance!

'Oh well,' thought Sid, 'I'll have to sort that out later. I'll just do some of my other garden jobs first.'

He hopped up onto the garden bench and looked at the messy wooden bird-table beside it. What a mess! Every single day it was completely covered in crumbs and bits of bread.

'Oh well,' thought Sid, 'I must do my share of the jobs and clear it all up.'

He quickly munched the bread and licked the table clean (while the birds looked on grumpily).

Next, Sid trotted down the garden path until he reached the washing line. There, on the line, was his special fluffy blanket waving around wildly in the autumn breeze.

'What's my blanket doing up there, blowing in the wind?' thought Sid. 'I must take it indoors before it flies away.'

He jumped up and grabbed it with his teeth, then dragged it through the muddy grass right up to the kitchen step.

'Mam will be pleased with me for helping,' he thought. But the kitchen door was closed, so he decided to leave the blanket right there on the step as a surprise for her.

'Right then,' thought Sid, 'now it's time to collect my favourite red ball.'

He passed Dad having a cup of tea as he marched down to the neat pile of leaves.

'Ready or not, here we go!' he yapped happily.

He dived onto the enormous pile of crunchy leaves and tunnelled through them, scattering them in all directions, until at last he found his special little ball. Boy, was he happy!

Then he scampered cheerfully up towards the house to show Geraint that he'd found his ball all by himself. Oh, Geraint would be so proud of him!

All of a sudden, he came to a stop. Geraint,
Mam and Dad were standing on the path
looking very confused and cross. What was
the matter? He sat and listened to them.

'How on earth did Sid's blanket get so
dirty, and how did it end up on the kitchen
step?' asked Mam.

Sid barked, 'It was me, Mam! I carried it up to the kitchen for you.'

But Mam just patted Sid's head, not really listening to him.

'I don't believe it,' moaned Dad. 'I'd just finished collecting all the leaves in the garden and it had taken me hours. Now look what the wind has done! It's blown them everywhere. What a mess!'

'Oh,' thought Sid, 'that wind was really naughty. Fancy blowing Dad's neat pile of leaves everywhere.' Well, he'd give Dad a hand later to sort out those leaves, *dim problem*.

'And just look at the empty bird-table. I think next door's cat has been eating the food that I put out for the birds again,' said Geraint. 'There are no crumbs left.'

Sid scurried around Geraint's legs, yapping away.

'No, Geraint, it was me! I've been clearing

it for you every single day because you're my best friend,' he barked.

Couldn't anybody see how useful he'd been all morning? Sid liked helping everyone with their jobs. He really felt like an important part of the family. It was just a pity that Mam and Dad and Geraint hadn't realised how much he'd done for them all that day.

Sid was very disappointed. So, he settled down in the sunshine and grumpily put his nose on his paws.

Chapter Two

Just then Dad asked Geraint if he wanted to play ball.

'What?' thought Sid, his ears pricking up. Geraint usually played ball with him, not Dad. What was going on? Had he heard right?

'Let's have a quick practice, Geraint. You've got a match this afternoon,' said Dad.

'Alright, I'll just get the ball,' answered Geraint.

'Get the ball! What does he mean?' thought Sid. Couldn't he see that Sid had his red ball safely tucked underneath his paw, ready and waiting?

But then, Geraint reappeared carrying a very strange looking ball. It wasn't round like Sid's. It wasn't red like Sid's. It was a very odd shape. It was big in the middle and small at both ends, and white. It looked like . . . a huge egg!

15

Sid sat in amazement as he watched Dad and Geraint kick the odd shaped white ball high in the air back and forth to each other.

They kicked and kicked the ball between each other, and it got muddier and muddier.

Feeling rather annoyed and left out of the game, he began to bark loudly to tell Dad and Geraint that he wanted to play too.

'Oh let me play! Let me join in! I want to catch the ball too,' thought Sid.

Then, Dad and Geraint started to throw the ball to each other. Sid leapt to his feet. This might be his chance. He jumped and jumped as high as he could. But each time he found that the ball was still too high for him to reach.

He barked his high pitched bark and ran as fast as he could, racing between Dad and Geraint, trying his best to catch the ball.

But, no matter how fast he ran, he just couldn't get quite close enough to get the ball. Dad and Geraint were too quick and too strong for him. His little legs quickly became tired, so he decided to sit glumly and watch for a while.

He had no chance of getting the ball. No chance at all, he thought.

Then, all of a sudden, Dad missed a catch! The ball rolled to the edge of the lawn. Sid couldn't believe his luck. This was his chance! He zoomed down the path, and quickly grabbed the ball as it made a final bounce and rolled beneath the apple tree. Somehow, Sid held it in his mouth and ran as fast as his short legs could carry him.

Chapter Three

'Come on Sid, give us the rugby ball back!' shouted Geraint, as he and Dad chased the little dog around the garden.

Oh wow! Sid really was part of this game now. He really was part of a proper game. He felt very important.

Once he'd run around the garden, up and down the path, around the washing line and vegetable patch too, he stopped, and saw that Dad was leaning against the wall, red faced and panting. Geraint was walking slowly towards him saying,

'*Whare teg*, fair play, Sid. You can run like the wind, boy. I didn't think that I'd ever catch up with you.'

With his little tail wagging like a flag, Sid ran back proudly to Geraint and dropped the ball by his feet.

Geraint stroked his smooth back and patted his head. Sid looked up at him, his tongue hanging out of one side of his mouth as he panted excitedly.

'*Da iawn*, good boy, Sid,' said Geraint, with a smile. 'We'll make a rugby player of you yet.'

'Geraint, you'd better go and get your rugby kit on, it's almost time for the game to start,' puffed Dad.

'Oops, all right,' replied Geraint, rushing into the house to get ready.

Sid lay in the sun again for a few minutes, full of pride at how amazing he'd been at playing rugby. Yes – with a bit more practice he could be a very useful player indeed, he thought, as he snoozed gently.

Moments later, Geraint appeared in his kit. Sid opened a bright eye and thought how smart his friend looked.

His shirt had a special badge on it to show that he was a member of the Cwmhendy rugby team. Very nice.

Sid suddenly wondered where his own kit was. Had Geraint forgotten that he needed to get ready too? He remembered that, somewhere, he too had a very smart T-shirt. Surely he would need it to go to the match? Geraint was in too much of a hurry to help him find it, so Sid had to go sniffing around for it by himself. That didn't take long. It was under the kitchen table.

He struggled to wriggle into the tiny top and whined when his head got stuck but, in the end, he managed it. He stood up and gazed into the mirror and thought that he looked very professional.

He was definitely one of the team now. Oh, he felt very important indeed.

When Geraint and Dad saw the little dog with short legs and curly pig's tail scamper into the room, wearing his own rugby kit, they laughed and patted his head.

'He's wearing my old rugby top,' said Geraint. 'The one that shrunk in the wash!'

'Oh Sid, you are a funny little dog,' added Dad. 'Let's get you out of that shirt now.'

'Oh, let him wear it, Dad,' said Geraint. 'He looks brilliant. I bet nobody else's dog will be wearing kit today!'

With a woof of pleasure, Sid wriggled happily into Geraint's arms and licked his chin, then off they went.

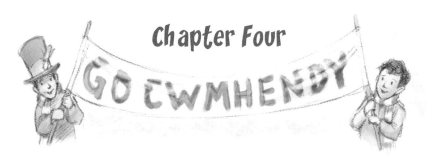

Chapter Four

Soon, they arrived at Cae Top playing fields, and Geraint ran off to find his team. There were crowds of people standing all around the pitch. They waved flags and banners as Geraint and his friends in the Cwmhendy team jogged onto the field.

Sid barked and pulled on his lead. He wanted to join them too, but Dad said firmly, 'Sorry Sid, only boys on the team. No dogs, I'm afraid.'

Sid sat sadly. He felt so disappointed. Didn't Dad understand that he and Geraint always played ball together? They were best friends. It didn't matter that he was a dog. It didn't matter at all. He gave a little sigh and lay down, and placed his head on his paws.

Then he heard a screeching sound. It was a whistle being blown. He watched in amazement as the ball was kicked up and down the pitch. Back and forth it went, very fast, until he felt quite confused. He didn't understand this game at all.

Usually, Geraint would throw the ball and then he would find it and bring it back. But this game was different. It didn't make any sense. Nobody, not one single boy, brought the ball back to Geraint's feet, the way he always did.

'Well, that's not very nice,' he thought. Poor Geraint. He felt so sorry for him because he never seemed to get the ball.

He whined and whined and pulled on his lead, begging Dad to let him go. Couldn't Dad see that Geraint needed his help to get that ball? Oh, why wouldn't he let him go?

Sid just knew that Geraint needed him at that moment, but Dad told him to 'Sit and be quiet.'

He did try. He sat at Dad's feet, resting his head on his shoes, and whimpered sadly at the unfairness of it all.

But he found it impossible to just sit and watch, when he felt he was needed so badly on the pitch. So, while Dad was chatting away to his mates and watching the game, Sid quietly wriggled his neck, and then his head and ears too, until eventually his collar slipped over his shiny black nose. He tip-toed gently away from Dad's feet, through the cheering crowds, until he finally reached the side lines on the other side of the field, where he could see Geraint playing.

He barked and barked, 'I'm here Geraint. Look over here! Can I play too?'

Geraint didn't see him. He didn't hear him either. But Dad did, and Dad looked cross. VERY cross indeed. He held the empty dog collar with the lead still attached high into the air, and shook it angrily.

Then, glaring, he started to walk around the pitch towards Sid.

Chapter Five

Sid tried to make himself look very small, as if he hadn't done anything wrong, but he knew that he'd been a bit naughty. He was a little bit sorry that he'd just sneaked off. Dad had probably been worried about where he was. He might even have thought that he was lost.

Feeling a bit scared, and knowing that Dad would be annoyed, Sid decided to hide. He looked around, searching for a good hiding place, but couldn't see anywhere.

Suddenly, he spotted an enormous sports bag lying on top of a little slope close to the pitch. He ran up beside it and saw that the zip was open just enough for him to hop inside. Without a moment's thought, he jumped in and snuggled deep inside the bag

so that nobody could see him. He stayed very, very still.

Just then, Dad arrived at the place where he'd spotted Sid. But of course, Sid was nowhere to be seen! Dad wondered where on earth the little dog had gone.

Hiding deep inside the bag, Sid suddenly felt a bit scared. It was dark and he was all alone. He needed to get out quickly so that he could see Geraint. He knew that he'd feel better then. He looked around for a way out, desperate to escape. But poor Sid just got caught up in a tangle of socks and towels, and couldn't find the opening.

From the outside, he could hear Dad calling his name over and over again. He was obviously worried.

'Sid! SID! Here boy! Where are you? SID!'

Sid jumped excitably inside the bag, eager to be at Dad's side.

All of a sudden, he felt the bag begin to slowly slip down the hillside. It moved faster and faster until, before long, it was tumbling over and over, rolling downwards at an incredible speed, with Sid's little legs running inside it like pistons. Down and down it rolled, until THUMP!

Eventually, the rolling stopped and Sid, who was feeling rather dizzy by now, found that the bag and its contents were now lying right on top of him.

Where on earth was he?

Then, he noticed that everything around him had become very quiet. The noisy cheering and shouting had stopped. What had happened?

A voice suddenly blasted out over the loud speaker. 'Well, well, I've seen it all now. We appear to have a giant tortoise on the pitch today! Stop the game, boys. Stop the game,' chuckled the commentator.

The crowd gasped, and then cheered as four small white legs and a curly pig's tail poked out of the bottom of the bag. Sid had

found his way out through the open zip and was pushing his way out onto the pitch.

'Oh, Sid! It just had to be you!' laughed Dad, running towards him.

Dad and Geraint untangled Sid from the towels and socks. The crowd roared with laughter as the little dog jumped up into Geraint's arms and barked and barked.

'It was you, Sid! We were all wondering how that sports bag managed to walk by itself. We had to stop the game,' giggled Geraint.

'Come on boy – back on your lead,' said Dad. 'No more escaping please.'

Chapter Six

Sid sat and let Dad replace his collar and lead him back to watch the game. He sat quietly like a good dog – until he noticed that the rugby game looked different somehow . . .

Everything seemed to change. Sid sat up quickly and saw that all the boys had stopped running around the pitch and were doing something very strange. He watched in wonder as he saw them all gather into a circle, then put their heads down as they

pushed and pulled and searched for the lost ball. That certainly looked dangerous for Geraint!

He yapped loudly, and Dad muttered,

'Shhhhh Sid, it's the scrum. Watch as they try and find the ball.'

He watched as patiently as he could, but no ball was found. No ball at all.

'That's it,' thought Sid. 'Enough's enough.'

He gently eased his collar over his head again and was off to join the game. He had to, because his help was needed – big time! He couldn't sit back a minute longer and watch them struggle to find that ball without his help. His skills were called for now.

He ran then, as fast as his little legs would go, until he reached the scrum.

He couldn't actually see Geraint, but he barked a message to him to let him know that he was on his way. He, Sid, the super incredible dog had arrived and he would

find the ball for Geraint. They were a team, they always helped each other.

So, when he saw a gap among the legs, he tunnelled his way through very bravely until he saw the odd shaped ball lying in the grass. He quickly pounced on it, and then grabbed it in his mouth, before running and running at full speed out of the scrum and onto the field.

He felt fantastic. He'd done it! He'd found the ball for Geraint.

He stopped for a second and his eyes searched the huge field for Geraint's face. So many people and faces!

Just as he was thinking what to do, he heard Dads voice calling.

Chapter Seven

'Sid! Sid, over here boy!'

Dad was standing next to the huge rugby posts, right at the end of the field.

'Oh well,' thought Sid, 'I'd better take the ball to Dad then. Perhaps Geraint is with him.'

He ran happily as fast as he could to Dad with the ball still in his mouth, and dropped the ball down as he crossed the white line painted on the grass.

As the referee blew his whistle again, he stopped in surprise. The crowd began to cheer and shout,

'The dog scored a try!'

'Si-id, Si-id' chanted everyone.

'Oh wow!' thought Sid. 'I've scored a try

– whatever that is. Everyone seems to be really happy for me.'

'Well done, Sid. But dogs can't score, sorry boy. Against the rules see. Only boys can play,' said Dad.

'Oh,' thought Sid. 'I hadn't been trying to score. I was just trying to help.'

Then he saw Geraint – his best friend in the whole world – who appeared amongst a group of boys looking all tired and muddy.

He ran towards Sid and lifted him up into the air. He hugged his little dog and said, 'Oh Sid, I'm so proud of you. You really wanted to help me, didn't you boy? That's what it's all about – teamwork. It doesn't matter that we didn't win. It was great fun wasn't it boy?'

Sid licked Geraint's muddy face until it looked quite clean.

Then the Cwmhendy team picked him up and lifted him into the air. Everyone called his name and sang.

'For Sid's a jolly good fellow, for Sid's a jolly good fellow, for Sid's a jolly good fellow – and so say all of us!'

He heard the coach say, 'Well Sid, I'm very impressed with the way you played today. So, I wonder if you would do us the honour of becoming our team mascot? You'll have to come to every game, mind, and support us with your wonderful enthusiasm. What do you say?'

'Well, well,' thought Sid, 'this is a VERY important job. This is much more important than helping with the washing and tidying the bird-table.'

He barked his reply instantly.

Yes, yes, he most definitely would love to be the team mascot. What an honour!

So now Sid goes to all the Cwmhendy

rugby matches as their team mascot. He wears a specially designed doggy rugby shirt as he trots proudly onto the pitch. And he starts every game, not with a whistle anymore but with his incredibly high pitched bark – over and over again!